Martin Meeker
and
Pauline Lagrande

Story by Else Breen
Illustrated by Vivian Zahl Olsen
English adaptation
by Amy Jo Cooper

Annick Press
Toronto, Canada

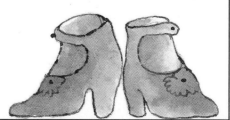

He was a grown man, but his legs dangled when he sat on a chair, or on the bus. That's how little he was. And although he never thought of himself as small, other people did. His size was all that anybody ever saw. Nobody ever bothered to find out more about him. Nobody bothered to ask him how he was, or what he thought. Who wants to waste their time bending down?

"Speak up," that's what people shouted at him.

"If you want a job, go out and grab one," was their well-intentioned advice.

"Be bold," said the self-help books.

"Anyone can get a job," they said at the employment centre.

"Try harder."

"Useless," was the general opinion.

Useless, that's how he felt.

But that didn't keep him from trying. Once a week he went to the employment centre. He might be little, but he had his methods. Every week, at the same time, Meeker—for that was his name, Martin Meeker—went down to the city, hoping at the employment centre he would find something useful to do.

"What do *you* want?" the young man at the reception desk asked him. When Meeker stated his request, as he did every time, the young man, who never seemed to remember him from week to week, sent him to Counter A. The people

at Counter A directed him to Counter B, where he waited for someone to notice him. But nobody wanted him.

Since no one would give him a job, Meeker had decided to give himself one. He had a typewriter at home. Nothing fancy, but it worked. Every morning, Meeker would get up, get dressed, have his coffee, sit at his typewriter and wait. He waited for his favourite time of day. He listened for the sound that gave him joy; the sound of the mail as it plopped in the mailbox.

Meeker always received piles of mail. Not personal letters, exactly. Meeker didn't really know that many people, and the people he did know lived nearby, so why would they write? What came in the mailbox every day were advertisements from people with things to sell.

Meeker made a job of reading the advertisements. He would make lists of the items for sale, compare prices, make notes.

But today he was too unhappy to even look at the mail. With a sigh, he lifted the lid of the mailbox and reached inside. There was the usual assortment of flyers. There was also an unusual looking letter. It had a a square cut out of it. A face smiled at him from the square. Meeker thought he had seen that face before. "Face in the box, now where have I seen that face in the box," Meeker muttered to himself. Then he realized. "How silly – of course."

Her name was Lagrande, an unusual name, and she was a singer on television. Right across the envelope, in big letters, were the words, "DO YOU WANT A JOB?"

"Yes," shouted Meeker, his heart leaping with joy. But there was more to read.

"Goodness!" Martin gasped as he read the second sentence. "What is the world coming to? Why would she want to be sold to a circus and want me, the smallest man in town, to do it?"

His hands shook but he managed to get the letter open. The paper was pink and smelled of roses. The handwriting was fancy, big and loopy, with circles instead of dots over the "i's". Meeker read it aloud.

My dear Mr. Meeker,
You are so very small, might I ask you just this one, tiny little favour? You see, not to go too much into detail, there has been a change. Or rather, to be more precise, I have changed. I am hardly myself. But enough about me. Let us just say that I want to try something new. Do you think, if you could find time in your tiny life, that you could sell me to a circus? If this sounds like a job you can do, please hasten to the above address as quickly as possible.

Yours ever so,
Lagrande

"A job, a job, somebody has given me a job," Meeker shouted and danced around the livingroom for joy. But imagine, he thought, selling people. The thought made him stop dancing. But only for a moment; because, he reasoned, a job is a job.

Meeker pulled on his coat and pushed his feet into his little boots. He was out the door and on his way to the address on the back of the envelope before he knew it. At last, someone had some use for him. At last, he could prove himself capable. That made him happy.

"What a beautiful day," Meeker sang aloud. "Listen to all the birds."

The houses on King's Road were very impressive, big and imposing. The biggest and most imposing was number 7 at the end of the street. It was so impressive, Meeker was not quite sure how to approach it. Should he ring the bell? What does one say to a famous person? Are there rules that Meeker was unaware of? Maybe he should just go back home.

The door finally opened. "Good afternoon, my name is . . . Heavens!" Meeker stepped back so far in his astonishment that he almost fell off the porch. For instead of a face, Meeker was staring straight at two huge female legs. Above his head somewhere dangled the hem of a skirt. Were there giant monsters living in this house?

From somewhere above a voice called down, "I hardly see what you have to be upset about. I'm up here, for heaven's sake. Look up, I'm in the skylight. I should think it only polite to look at the person who's talking to you."

He looked up and sure enough, there was Lagrande's pretty head sticking out of the skylight, tears pouring down her face, down the roof, and on to Meeker. As he looked at her, large and sobbing, Meeker felt the smallest and most helpless he had ever felt in his entire life. He also wished he had brought his umbrella.

"How did you get so big?" Meeker managed to stammer.

"I hardly think this is the place to discuss my situation. Come in and close the door. We will discuss it inside. I'll bend down and come inside, too."

Meeker thought there was something familiar about Lagrande's posture as she sat there bent double in a corner of the room. Something uncomfortably familiar.

"I didn't realize you were *that* small," Lagrande said seeing Meeker close up. "Whatever have they done to you?"

"I grew up under the kitchen table," said Meeker; "Little room for expansion. You are lucky that you have a whole house. But if you don't mind my saying so, if you plan to grow any more, the house will soon be too small for you. You're a bit of a tight fit already, if you know what I mean."

"Must you rub it in?" cried Lagrande shaking the house with her sobs. "As if I

were not aware of it already. The last time I was on television, the producers said that they didn't want to see me until I was a more reasonable size."

Meeker had to admit that he had never heard anything like that, it was true. But he was dying of curiosity—the idea of growth always made him curious—so he asked, perhaps a bit impolitely, "What do people say when they see you in the streets?"

Lagrande sniffed, "Well, I just don't let them see me. How could I? I don't go out. Of course, it doesn't matter if *you* see me. I mean, you're so small," she added. "And I do have a secretary who mails all of my letters and makes my arrangements. Or, rather, I did have a secretary," Lagrande corrected herself. "She left today. No notice, just walked right out. And her reason? She said she didn't like people who got too big. She said it was unpleasant being around them. Unpleasant! How can she say that when it is me who's having such a hard time." Lagrande broke out in a fresh round of tears.

Meeker waited for her sobs to subside and then, in a quiet voice, asked, "Are you sure about that? About the hard time?"

Lagrande stopped crying and glowered at him. "Do you think I enjoy being folded up like an accordion?"

"It's just..." Meeker hesitated, trying to be delicate. "It's just that when people get so terribly big, they take up so much space that there is little room for smaller – or perhaps I should say, people who are not quite as big as you are."

Then a thought, which he didn't mean to think, but which appeared anyway, made Meeker giggle.

"Well, I'm glad you find me amusing," Lagrande said, deeply offended.

"No, it's just..." Meeker mumbled. How could he explain? An image had popped into his mind of a streetcar full of people the size of Lagrande. People so big they had to squeeze themselves into awkward positions to fit, while he, at his size, was able to cling to one of them by

the belt and support himself as the streetcar rattled and wound along its track. A silly thought; it was probably best to keep it to himself. Lagrande might not find it as

funny. So instead he asked, "And just when, and how, did you start growing?"

Lagrande sighed, and even in her bigness she suddenly looked small, unsure if she could trust him. Meeker nodded. "You can tell me."

"Every time they told me how big I was, I believed them. I mean, I wanted to believe they were right. Somebody would say, 'You're big, baby' or 'you're the tops, sweetheart', and I would grow. Well, at first I didn't pay much attention. A little height can only help. The day they made me world famous, I banged my head on the ceiling. That's when the producer said: 'We can't show you anymore. You're too big for us.' I was no longer any use to them."

Meeker nodded. He knew about being useless. He also thanked his lucky stars for being too small rather than too big. At least when you are too small, nobody notices you. A person can't hide the fact that they are too big.

She sat stuffed in the corner of the room looking sad and lost. Meeker gazed around. On every wall, full colour posters of Lagrande—smiling her most charming smile—were plastered over all the available space. On every poster, in giant print, the same word appeared:

THE GREATEST

"What do they mean by that?" Meeker asked.

Lagrande shook herself out of her thoughts of misery and looked where Meeker was pointing. "Oh, that," she said casually; "they mean that I'm the best in the whole wide world. If they repeat it often enough, everybody will believe it."

"But that can't be true," Meeker protested. "It's impossible to tell who is the best of all in the whole world."

"How do you know?" Lagrande asked sharply.

"You can't believe what you read in an advertisement."

"You can't?"

"No, they say everything is the greatest or the best or number one." Meeker recited, "'the best vacuum cleaner money can buy'; 'the number one back support'; 'the greatest vegetable scrubber in the world.' What are you the greatest at, by the way?" Meeker smiled, a bit condescending perhaps.

Lagrande had to look at the poster. She read, "I'm 'the most beautiful' and '... probably the best singer of our times.'"

"Sounds like these posters feed your growth problem. Shall I take them down?"

"If you think it will help."

Meeker nodded. He tore down all the posters, rolled them up and put all but one of them in the fireplace. "I'll need something to show them at the circus. I mean, if you still want me to sell you."

"Oh yes, please." Lagrande brightened up. "There is a circus in town right now. I want you to go to the manager and offer my services as the most beautiful and the biggest lady in the world."

"Careful, careful." Meeker was wor-

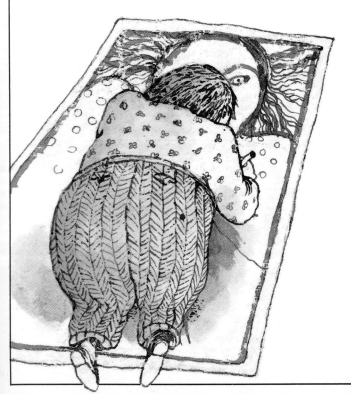

ried. "I think you just grew a bit. You can't get too big. How tall are you, anyway?"

"Three metres eighty." Lagrande heaved a sigh and wiped an errant tear with the table cloth which was just the right size for a handkerchief.

"Well, we'll just have to make sure you don't grow any more than that." Meeker took a red felt pen and crossed out the words 'THE GREATEST'. In its place he wrote:

THREE METRES
　EIGHTY :
　BEAT THAT!

Things were not great at the circus. The clown had tripped over his own shoelaces and broken his leg; the doctor said it would take six weeks to heal. A clown in a cast is not funny. The circus manager was beside himself. He would probably have to cancel the show. Or else, replace the clown. But how?

"Now what! Now what!" the circus manager pondered as he sat at his desk under the big top eating jellybabies.

"There's a little man outside who would like to speak with you," the animal trainer informed him.

"What?" The circus manager tore himself away from his thoughts. "No, no, I'm much too busy. Tell him to wait. Too busy to talk." The circus manager waved him away and munched another jellybaby.

Little men are used to waiting. So Meeker sat. But after an hour he felt that he had waited long enough.

Inside the tent it was quiet and dark. It smelled of sawdust, peanuts, and remotely of elephants. Behind a curtain which separated the ring from the rest of the tent sat the circus manager. Meeker pulled the curtain aside and made a little noise in his throat, to let the manager know that he was there.

"Go away. Can't you see I'm busy," the manager growled without turning around.

"Excuse me." Meeker became just a bit more forceful.

"I said go . . . " the manager turned around. His face changed to a bright smile. He leapt from his chair. "I mean, good day, my little man. You are just what I'm looking for. Dear, dear, you should have said it was you. Have a jellybaby."

"No, thank you." Meeker could see that the man was confused. So he explained, "No, it's someone else you want," and he pushed the rolled-up poster so closely under the manager's nose that the man had to take a few steps backwards.

"THREE METRES EIGHTY: BEAT THAT!" the circus manager read slowly. He couldn't believe his luck. The circus was saved. The manager was so happy that he jumped up, ran into the ring and did a triple somersault, much to Meeker's amazement.

"Lucky for me," the circus manager mumbled to himself, but then more loudly to Meeker, "How fortunate, because I'm looking for big people, or tiny ones; humongous ones, or skinny ones. You, for instance, are perfect!" The manager poked at Meeker with his finger.

Meeker was a bit ruffled. "I'm a normal person. Just a bit on the small side. I have no desire to be exhibited in a circus."

"Nobody said you were abnormal, my dear man," the circus manager said soothingly, "but you would reconsider, perhaps, if there were a little extra offered." The manager smiled, rubbing his fingers together.

"What do you mean by 'extra'?" Meeker asked.

"Why money, of course." The manager's smile was so wide by now, it almost split his face in two.

Meeker was not tempted by money. He had all he needed.

"I'm acting on behalf of Lagrande. I'm here to get her a job." Meeker firmly set his lips. "And you can't just buy her, either. It is a business deal. We will need a contract. I want everything above board."

"Of course, of course," said the manager bowing and bowing, "whatever you say."

An hour later, Meeker left the circus very pleased with how he had handled the job. He stood outside the big top with two contracts and his pockets stuffed full of jellybabies. One contract required Lagrande's services as a circus performer; the other required Meeker's services as an animal keeper. Not quite what Meeker had bargained for, but in all business negotiations, there has to be compromise.

"A decent agreement," Meeker thought, "but you can't trust anything until you've actually signed the contract, sealed the deal. A lot can happen before then."

And how right he was.

It was a beaming Lagrande who opened the door for him. Her outlook had changed. "Guess what!" she cried excitedly, before Meeker could even say 'hello'. "I'm shrinking. Can't you tell?"

How could Meeker not tell! Lagrande now fit in her house, although she still looked as if she were walking on stilts.

"As long as you don't get too small for the work I've arranged for you. It's a big job." He put the contracts on the table for her to read. "You see, you'll be a circus performer—two shows a day—and I'm hired to look after the animals. A good profession, that. I'm not complaining."

But his feet were. They ached so that he had to sit in the nearest chair. His boots felt way too small.

Lagrande looked Meeker carefully up and down.

"Funny," she said, "perhaps it's nothing. It's probably my imagination, but you seem taller to me. Maybe because I'm not as big as before. It's just the perspective." A worried look appeared on her face. "Tell me. You don't think you've got the growth bug, have you? I mean, just a bit?"

Meeker looked in amazement at his feet which were firmly planted on the floor. Goodness, he *had* grown.

"Oh dear. I hope that illness of yours isn't contagious." The thought of growing out of proportion scared Meeker.

"Oh, don't be such a ninny! It would do you good to stretch some. You really aren't such a small man, you know."

"It's just that I don't want to get too big for myself, if you know what I mean."

Lagrande looked offended, then sad. She knew what he meant.

"Never mind that," Meeker said. "Have a look at the contract. Read it carefully because the circus manager is coming tomorrow and he'll want us to sign."

"You've been so enormously clever." The sight of the contract cheered Lagrande right up.

Meeker left. He wanted to buy some clothes that fit him.

An impatient ring woke Meeker from his sleep the next morning. It took him a moment to realize someone was at the door. Throwing on his new clothes, Meeker went to see who wanted him so early in the morning. On the porch was a man with a camera around his neck and a pad and pencil in his hand.

"Daily News," the man said, "I'm here to cover a story on a guy called Meeker. Is he in?"

Meeker yawned, "Yes, yes, I'm Meeker."

The reporter shook his head. "No, the guy I want is little: a regular shrimp."

"I *am* Meeker, I tell you!"

The reporter looked around to make sure no one would overhear what he was going to say. Then he leaned close and whispered confidentially, "This Meeker is so small, he is going to star in the circus. That's why I'm here. I want to get a picture."

The nerve! thought Meeker. There was nothing in the contracts about performing. That circus manager must think he's pretty smart. We'll see about that. Meeker opened his mouth to say something, but snapped it shut again in amazement. Something was wrong. No, not wrong, different. He was looking the reporter right in the eyes. Eye to eye!

Without saying a word, he pushed the reporter aside and ran all the way to No. 7 King's Road.

Impatiently he knocked on the door. Lagrande was slow to open it, but when she did, it was just as he had suspected. Lagrande was a normal height, the same size she was before she started to grow. Her problem had vanished. She threw her arms around Meeker—further proof of her full recovery—and called him her best friend ever. That was something she would never dream of doing when she was too big.

Now it was Lagrande's turn to be amazed. She held Meeker at arm's length and looked at him closely.

"You're not small anymore."

"No, I don't seem to be, do I?" Meeker didn't know whether to be happy or sad. "I wonder what caused it."

"You would be the best judge of that," Lagrande told him.

Meeker nodded. It must have something to do with his new job. Then a thought made him panic: "What if I don't stop growing?"

Lagrande laughed, "Then it'll be your turn to stand with your head in the sky-light." She stopped laughing when she saw Meeker's face. "Listen, don't worry," she comforted him. "You're not the kind of person who will get too big. You'll stay for breakfast?"

Of course he would. He had run out of the house so quickly, he had not even been able to eat a piece of toast.

They were just about to sit down at the table when they heard a terrible commotion outside. Lagrande decided to investigate. When she opened the door, in tumbled the circus manager, together with the reporter. They were both talking at once, trying to out-shout each other.

"Don't mess with me, buddy." The reporter shook his finger at the circus manager.

"But I tell you, it's true. You went to the wrong place," the circus manager shouted.

"Well, this is the place *you* wanted. Look around. See anything unusual? I don't. I just see two perfectly normal looking people."

The circus manager looked around. He looked behind him. He looked in front of him. He looked up. He looked down. He didn't even say 'hello'; instead, he looked again. He scratched his head. "Does a woman by the name of Lagrande live here? Very big, you can't miss her."

"What does it say on the door?" Meeker asked him.

"No. 7," answered the circus manager, a little confused by the question.

"Well, there you are then. That's that, isn't it," said Meeker, pleased with himself.

"You've been tricked," the reporter said, not without some satisfaction.

"But where are my precious performers? My little cherub? The great angel, Lagrande, who was to save my circus?" The manager was crestfallen.

"The name's Pauline, by the way," said Lagrande with mild surprise. When she said 'Pauline', there was a faint snap, as if something were settling back into its right place. Meeker heard it and smiled.

"I've got something to hold on to," Pauline whispered excitedly to Meeker, "my name. Did you hear?"

But the circus manager was not satisfied. "You know," he told her, squinting, "I could swear you were that television singer. The one that got too big."

"Knock it off, will you," the reporter was losing his patience, "can't you see that she's just trying to be a look-alike? And she's not doing a very good job at it either. I mean the hair . . . it's all wrong."

Pauline had to turn her face to hide her grin.

"What about him, then?" the reporter asked, pointing at Meeker. "Next I suppose you'll try to tell me that this is the littlest man in town, the one who is to star in your circus."

Meeker immediately sat down on the chair, as if he were suddenly overcome with the need to have breakfast.

The reporter stared at Meeker. "Didn't I talk with you earlier? Are you a relative or something of that little guy? What is your name, anyway?"

"Martin," said Meeker, deciding first names were okay.

The circus manager was more than confused. "You're not him," he sighed, shaking his head. "I mean the face, perhaps. But Meeker was a small man, in tiny boots and a little coat. A man who didn't know the first thing about business: a trusting man. He came to me with a poster of a woman three metres eighty. But where can they be?"

"A poster? I can't believe you fell for a poster!" The reporter was laughing so hard, his camera bobbed up and down on his belly. "You've been had, buddy."

"But I tell you, I saw him with my own eyes. He was so little, he could barely scratch my ear. And the contracts. We drew up two contracts which we were supposed to sign here today."

The reporter bellowed with laughter, "Of all the old tricks . . . he probably gave you the wrong address. Seems to me it's you who doesn't know about business, buddy."

The circus manager fumed. Pauline was fed up.

"This is all very amusing, but some people do have breakfast in the morning. Do you mind?" And she escorted the pair, still squabbling, out the door.

"Well, good riddance," Pauline said, wiping her hands.

Martin smiled at her slyly. Then he got up slowly, revealing the contracts he had been sitting on. Pauline smiled back.

"Good thing we didn't sign these things. What a crook that guy is," Martin said.

"True. I'd rather be unemployed than work for him," Pauline agreed.

So they rolled up the poster, tore up the contracts and threw everything into the fire. Their problems were solved. They had recovered.

They took their breakfast outside, because it was the sort of day that demanded breakfast outside—blue skies, singing birds, flowers blooming—you know what I mean.

Then and there, right in the garden, Pauline hired Martin. She wanted him to act as a consultant, on letter writing. She had decided to go into business for herself.

"Do you think we'll get work?" Pauline asked, reaching for more bread. "We are still both unemployed."

"Self-employed," Martin corrected her. "I've got just the project. We'll tell your story; all about your growth problem. This way, the circus manager, the reporter and everyone else will know what really happened. We can sell the story to a publisher. We must remember to retain the movie rights. I'll make a note of that."

"Excellent idea," Pauline cheered. "Let's get started right away."

And they did. Right after breakfast, Martin went home for his typewriter. He strolled along, looking over the garden fences with contentment, taking long, even strides. He could see so much more now that he was as tall as everyone else.

He returned to No. 7 King's Road with his typewriter. There, in the garden, the true story of MARTIN MEEKER AND PAULINE LAGRANDE was written.

Should anyone who reads this be infected by the same ailment as Pauline or Martin, remember that the complaint is not entirely uncommon. Many people are affected. But don't worry, you can recover. There is always a cause for the problem, but you will discover these things yourself.

First published by Aschehoug, Oslo
Original title Morten Minus og Pauline Plus

Annick Press Ltd.
All rights reserved
Foreign Rights:
Kerstin Kvint Agency
Stockholm, Sweden

Canadian Cataloguing in Publication Data

Breen, Else.
    Martin Meeker and Pauline Lagrande

Translation of: Morten minus og Pauline Plus.
ISBN 1-55037-065-0 (bound). – ISBN 1-55037-064-2 (pbk.)

I. Olsen, Vivian Zahl. II. Title.

PZ54.5.B74Ma 1989   j839.8′2374   C89-094030-4

Distributed in Canada and the USA by:
Firefly Books Ltd.
250 Sparks Avenue
Willowdale, Ontario
M2H 2S4

Printed and bound in Canada